S0-BBG-101

For Marilyn:
Mom – Thank you for showing me how to see the world as an explorer and a dreamer.
–A.K.

In memory of my precious mother whose unconditional love blessed me for a lifetime.
–J.N.

Copyright Andi King, 2016
All rights reserved

ISBN: 978-0-578-14073-5

Princess of the Pines

Written by Andi King

Illustrated by Jerry Novotny

One sunny day, Andrea looked out her bedroom window.

Pine trees moved back and forth in the wind, and there were tall mountains in the distance.

The breeze blowing in though the window screen smelled of pinecones and wildflowers.

Andrea loved her home in Pine Grove, but she dreamed of exploring the world. She wanted adventure.

"Take your daydreaming outside," Andrea's mom said. "Daydreams lead to adventure, so go outside and play. Find your adventure exploring the mountains and trees."

Andrea grabbed her pinecone tiara and set out in search of an adventure. Along the way, she found a branch and decided it would make the perfect magic wand to take her anywhere she wanted to go.

She walked up the road lined with pine trees to the fire tower that overlooked the Sierra Nevada Mountains.

Today, just for her, the fire tower would be the Eiffel Tower. She closed her eyes and pointed her wand at the tower. Take me to Paris, France!

When she opened her eyes, instead of the fire tower, the Eiffel Tower was in front of her. A French girl wearing a beret was walking her dog. "*Bonjour*! Where are you from?" The French girl asked.

Andrea replied, "*Bonjour*! I'm from Pine Grove, California in the United States of America."

bonjour [bawn-zhoor] - hello

"What is it like there?" asked the French girl.

"It's in the mountains and the wind rushes around the pine trees just like the wind rushes around the Eiffel Tower."

The French girl said, "That sounds lovely. Maybe I will travel there someday," and gave Andrea her beret as a keepsake.

"*Merci*," Andrea said and waved as the French girl walked away saying, "*Au revoir!*"

merci [mer-see] – thank you
au revoir [oh ruh-vwahr] – goodbye

Back at the fire tower, Andrea walked down the hill to a tree leaning across the path. Today, just for her, it would be the Leaning Tower of Pisa. She closed her eyes and pointed her wand at the tree. Take me to Pisa, Italy!

When she opened her eyes, instead of the leaning tree, the Leaning Tower of Pisa was in front of her. An Italian girl wearing a handkerchief on her head waved to her, "*Buongiorno*! Where are you from?"

Andrea said, "*Buongiorno*!" and told her.

buongiorno [bwawn jawr-naw] – Hello

"What is it like there?" asked the Italian girl.

"It's in the mountains and there are trees that grow straight and tall but some lean just like the Leaning Tower of Pisa."

The Italian girl said, "It sounds interesting. Maybe I will travel there someday," and gave Andrea her handkerchief as a keepsake.

"*Grazie*," Andrea said and waved as the Italian girl walked away saying, "*Ciao!*"

grazie [gra-tsje] – thank you
ciao [chah-aw] – goodbye

Back at the leaning tree, Andrea looked up the hill and saw Mr. Lukens. He waved from the footbridge that went across the stream in front of his log cabin. He reminded Andrea of a knight in shining armor guarding a castle. Today, just for her, Mr. Lukens' cabin would be a Spanish castle. She closed her eyes and pointed her wand. Take me to Segovia, Spain!

When she opened her eyes, instead of Mr. Lukens' cabin, Segovia Castle was in front of her.

A Spanish girl with a red flower in her hair walked up to her. "*Hola*! Where are you from? Do you live near a castle like me?"

Andrea said, "*Hola*! I live in the mountains in California where some houses have bridges over streams in front of them, so I pretend they are castles."

hola [oh-lah] - hello

The Spanish girl said, "It sounds magical. Maybe I will travel there someday," and gave Andrea her red flower as a keepsake.

"*Gracias*," Andrea said and waved as the Spanish girl walked away saying, "*Adios!*"

gracias [grah-see-uhs] – thank you
adios [ad-ee-ohs] – goodbye

Back at the cabin, Andrea waved goodbye to Mr. Lukens. She ran along the stream and then hopped across it on round stepping-stones.

She stopped to look at a sundial in a neighbor's yard. Today, just for her, it would be Big Ben. She closed her eyes and pointed her wand at the sundial, "Take me to London, England!"

When she opened her eyes, instead of the sundial, Big Ben was in front of her.

"Bong! Bong! Bong!" Big Ben chimed.

An English girl wearing a royal dress and a diamond tiara asked, "Where are you from, Princess?"

Andrea said, "I live where the pine trees grow tall and the wind whispers around the mountains, but I live in a house, not a castle. I'm not a real princess, but sometimes I daydream that I am one just like you."

"Well, you look like a princess," the English girl said pointing to Andrea's pinecone tiara. "I will call you, Princess of the Pines."

Andrea liked that very much. She hugged her new princess friend, and they exchanged tiaras.

Back in Pine Grove, the sun was setting and the wind seemed to be whispering, "home...home...home." Andrea was tired from her adventures and decided there was no other place she wanted to go today but home.

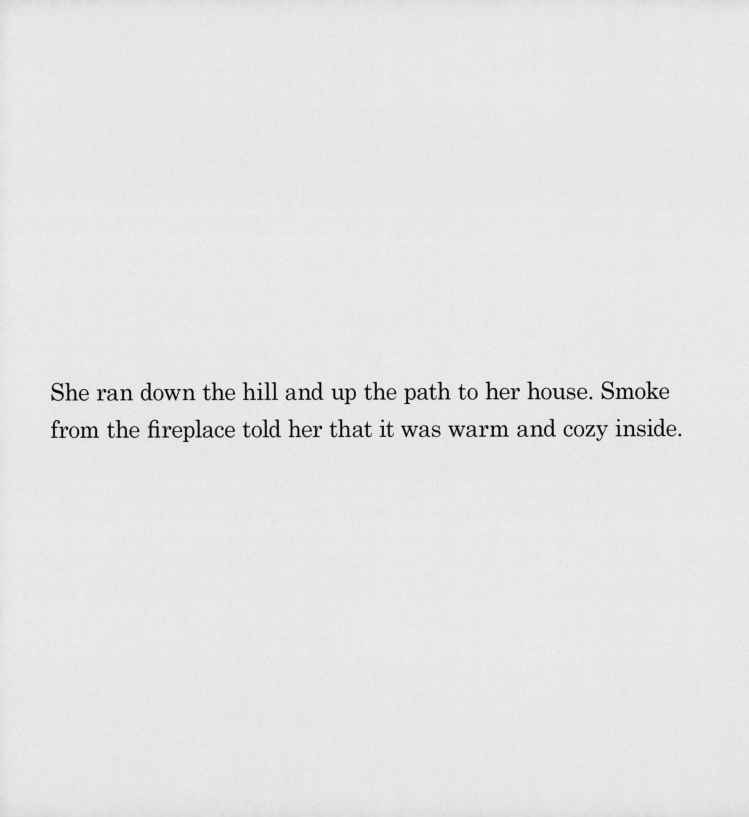

She ran down the hill and up the path to her house. Smoke from the fireplace told her that it was warm and cozy inside.

When she opened the door, she could smell chocolate chip cookies. Her mom asked, "How was your adventure?"

Andrea told her mom about the fire tower, the leaning tree, Mr. Lukens' cabin, and the sundial. She explained that she used her magic wand to change them into exciting places and that she made friends from different countries.

Her mom gave Andrea a big hug and said, "I'm very happy you found adventure. Someday when you are older, you will have all of those adventures and more. Until then, here's a warm cookie for the Princess of the Pines."

Made in the USA
Coppell, TX
08 April 2021

53326548R00031